A MESSAGE TO PARENTS

It is of vital importance for parents to read good books to young children in order to aid the child's psychological and intellectual development. At the same time as stimulating the child's imagination and awareness of his environment, it creates a positive relationship between parent and child. The child will gradually increase his basic vocabulary and will soon be able to read books alone.

Brown Watson has published this series of books with these aims in mind. By collecting this inexpensive library, parent and child are provided with hours of pleasurable and profitable reading.

© 1995 Brown Watson
ENGLAND
Printed and bound in Germany

Teddy's
Birthday Surprise

by Maureen Spurgeon
Illustrated by Pamela Storey

Brown Watson
ENGLAND

Teddy Bear woke up, blinking at the sun shining into his room. Birds sang and chattered noisily. Downstairs, Mummy and Daddy Bear laughed and talked together. But why did it feel a special sort of day?

"My birthday!" he remembered, jumping out of bed.

He hoped he would have lots of birthday cards, and Mummy and Daddy always let him open his presents at breakfast-time.
"Happy Birthday, Teddy!" called Mummy Bear.

"Many happy returns!" smiled Daddy. Teddy said nothing. There was one card beside his plate, but no presents – not even from Uncle Sailor Bill. And he never forgot birthdays!

"Cheer up!" smiled Daddy Bear.
"You might have a special
birthday surprise later on."
"A birthday party?" cried Teddy.
"Like last year?"

He had loved blowing up lots of balloons and hanging them all around the room. But Mummy shook her head. "No, Teddy," she said. "Not a birthday party."

"Maybe Mummy and Daddy haven't enough money to spend on parties and birthdays," thought Teddy.
He opened the card, and up popped a little bear, smiling and waving at him!

"That's your first birthday surprise," laughed Daddy.
Teddy Bear did like the card! He took it out into the garden, opening and closing it again and again.

Suddenly, he saw his friend Barry Bear. "Hello, Barry!" he cried. "It's my birthday today, and I've got . . ."

"Can't stop, Teddy!" Barry called back. "See you later!"

Teddy couldn't help being surprised. Where COULD Barry be going in such a hurry that he didn't have time to stop and talk? He had never done such a thing before.

Teddy was about to go back
indoors, when he saw Teacher
Bear carrying a basket and two
shopping bags. They looked very
heavy. "Do you need any help,
Teacher Bear?" he asked.

"Er – no thank you, Teddy," she said quickly. "I – I think I can manage." And off she went down the road just as fast as she could. Teddy Bear was surprised all over again.

Next minute, the sparrows and robins flew down and began pecking at some sausage roll crumbs on the ground. Teddy knew that they must have fallen

from Teacher Bear's basket.
"I wonder where Teacher Bear was taking those sausage rolls?" thought Teddy.
He loved sausage rolls! He was still wondering when he heard voices by the back gate.

It was Honey Bear and Tiny Bear!
"Hurry up, you two," said Honey's
mummy, "or we won't get it all
finished in time!"
"Get WHAT finished in time?"
Teddy wanted to know.

But they just went past, Honey Bear's mummy pushing her shopping trolley with a big box on top. By now, Teddy was sure something was going on, something he didn't know about.

Then he heard voices whispering his name! "Is that you, Billy Bear?" he called out. And sure enough, the cheeky face of Billy Bear peeped out from behind a big tree.

"Oh – er, hello, Teddy," he
said. "Er – we were just going
somewhere, weren't we, Bella?"
Bella was Billy's sister.
"What have you got behind your
back?" asked Teddy.

"Me?" said Billy. "Nothing!" And he and Bella ran off just as fast as they could go!

"Hey!" shouted Teddy, loud enough for Mummy and Daddy to hear. "Come back!"

"What's wrong?" asked Mummy.
"I just don't know!" sighed Teddy.
And he told them all that had
happened. "Billy and Bella
wouldn't even say where they
were going!" he finished.

"Why don't we go the same way?" Daddy Bear suggested. "We might find out, then."
So, they went along the path. Suddenly, Teddy saw something through the trees . . .

It was a bunch of balloons,
bobbing in the breeze, with
streamers and paper lanterns!
Then came the sound of a guitar
and voices began to sing, "Happy
Birthday to You!"

"Happy Birthday, dear Teddy!
Happy Birthday to you!" Teddy
was so surprised, he couldn't
speak! All his friends were there,
even Uncle Sailor Bill!

"Mummy had your birthday cake when you saw us!" laughed Honey. "Teacher Bear made the sausage rolls, and Tiny and I brought the balloons!"

"And look at all your presents!" smiled Barry Bear.
"It's a birthday picnic with games to follow!" said Mummy. "We will all have such fun!"